If I Forget Thee

TO THE HAGANAH

whose men and women of Palestine found their way into Europe by parachute and later by every imaginable means, their mission being to bring survivors home.

If I Forget

A PICTURE STORY OF

PHOTOGRAPHS BY P. GOLDMAN, SASHA ALEXANDER, AND OTHERS, BASED ON THE FILM *MY FATHER'S HOUSE*, PRODUCED IN PALESTINE BY HERBERT KLINE AND MEYER LEVIN, DIRECTED BY HERBERT KLINE, AND PHOTOGRAPHED BY FLOYD CROSBY.

Thee

ODERN PALESTINE

by MEYER LEVIN

New York • The Viking Press • 1947

Other Books by Meyer Levin

REPORTER
FRANKIE AND JOHNNY
YEHUDA

THE NEW BRIDGE
THE GOLDEN MOUNTAIN
THE OLD BUNCH

CITIZENS
MY FATHER'S HOUSE

Photographs in This Book by:

P. GOLDMAN: Pages 6, 7, 8, 8a, 9, 11, 12, 13, 15, 17, 17a, 18, 19, 20, 21, 22, 23, 26, 26a, 27, 28a, 29, 29a, 31, 33, 34, 34a, 35, 37, 39, 40, 40a, 41, 42a, 44, 45, 46, 47, 47a, 48, 48a, 49, 50, 51, 52, 53, 55, 55a, 56, 56a, 63, 64, 65, 66, 66a, 67, 68, 71, 75, 76, 78, 122a, 126, 126a, 127, 128 128a, 131 131a, 132, 133, 133a, 134, 135, 135a, 136, 136a, 137, 137a, 138, 141, 142, 143.

SASHA ALEXANDER: Pages 32, 41a, 42, 43, 69, 69a, 82a, 83, 83a, 84, 87, 87a, 88, 91, 91a, 97, 98, 99, 100, 113, 113a, 114, 114a, 115, 115a, 116, 118, 120, 120a, 121, 122, 123, 124, 125, 129, 129a, 130.

TRUDI SCHWARTZ: Pages 38, 59, 60, 60a, 70, 70a, 85, 86, 90, 102, 103, 104, 105, 105a, 106, 107, 108a, 109, 111, 111a, 112, 112a, 117, 118a, 118b, back of jacket.

FLOYD CROSBY: Title page, pages 30, 57, 58, 72, 77, 77a, 82, 92a, 93, 96, 119.

ROBERT ZILLER: Front of jacket, pages 14, 16, 24, 24a, 25, 25a, 28, 44a, 78a, 81a.

ROLPH KNOELLER: Pages 16a, 57a, 61, 71a, 74, 79, 80, 80a, 124a.

BEN OYSERMAN: Pages 31a, 92, 93, 95, 101.

MEYER LEVIN: Pages 10, 10a, 19a, 35a, 36, 54, 58a, 61a, 62, 73, 81, 88a, 89, 94, 94a, 96a, 108, 110, 110a, 134a, 139, 140.

(A letter following a page number indicates a small picture on that page.)

COPYRIGHT 1947 BY MEYER LEVIN

FIRST PUBLISHED BY THE VIKING PRESS IN NOVEMBER 1947

PUBLISHED ON THE SAME DAY IN THE DOMINION OF CANADA
BY THE MACMILLAN COMPANY OF CANADA LIMITED

PRINTED IN U.S.A. BY PHOTOGRAVURE AND COLOR COMPANY

IN DESIGNING this picture story we hoped to make better known a new-old thing in this world: the life of the Jews in Palestine.

Through the action of the country itself upon a human life in crisis, we felt we could show the ways of the collective settlements, and of the factories, and of the cities. We wished to show how the land is in Galilee, and on the Sharon shore, and by the Dead Sea, and in the desert of the Negev, and how life moves in the modern cities of Haifa and Tel Aviv, and in the old and new Jerusalem.

The settlement of Makor Galil is a composite of the settlements of Maabaroth, Afikim, Kiryat Anavim, Ramat Rachel, Givat Chayim, and others. The people in the settlements and in the cities are always the people of the place, doing as they do in their daily life. The builders of the new colony in the desert are the youth group of Kibbutz Nirrim, putting up their settlement.

We found no one who could not act because we did not want people to act. We wanted people to show the lives that they know. And to the participants this film was a welcome instrument for bringing out to the world much that they felt needed to be truly known.

On a moonless night, a refugee ship was met by the Haganah.

[7]

[8]

Among the first to land was a boy who searched the faces of all the Palestinians. "Isn't my father here?" he asked of the Haganah leader. "My father said I would find him in Palestine. My name is David Halevi."

"We'll find him," the Haganah leader, Avram, promised.

David had a friend, Big Stepan, who wanted first of all to feel the earth of Palestine that was under the stones.

As they mounted the truck that waited in a near-by grove, Stepan reached and took fruit from a tree.

"What is it?" David asked.

"An orange. An orange of Judea!" Stepan said.

[10]

Before dawn they passed Mount Tabor, on the plain known as Emek Israel—the Valley of Israel.

They crossed the little country in a few hours.

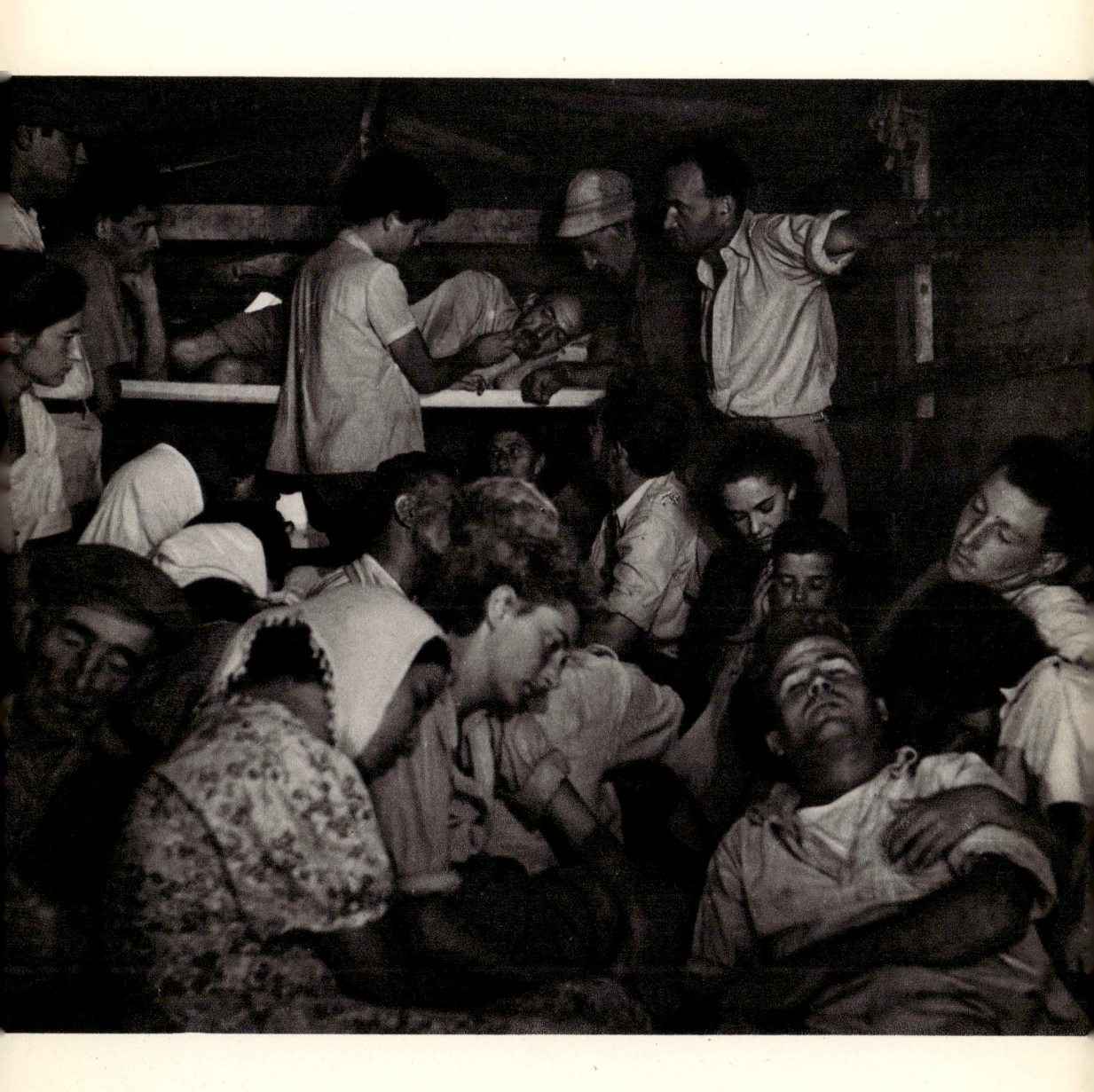

[12]

David sat with Marta, who had become his friend on the ship.

Big Stepan and young Dvora were together.

They came to the Sea of Galilee. In Hebrew, the Palestinians told them, this sea is called Kinnereth, from the word *kinor,* which means a violin.

The truck was stopped while Avram went to make sure that the way past the police station was clear. Now for the first time the tarpaulin was lifted, and the refugees saw the land to which they had come to live.

[16]

Thus the survivors approached the collective settlement of Makor Galil —the Root of Galilee.

The watchman on the water tower of the settlement was on the lookout for the truck. "They are safe!" he shouted.

Abba, the eldest of the settlers and the father of Avram, rode out to meet the newcomers.

The Palestinians at their early tasks knew that the Haganah's night mission was accomplished.

As the gong sounded, the people of Makor Galil dropped their work and ran to welcome the refugees.

"Is there anyone from Budapest?"

"From Frankfort?"

"From Lublin?" "Dessau?" "Vienna?" "Warsaw?"

The names of cities and towns in all of Europe echoed back and forth between the settlers and the survivors.

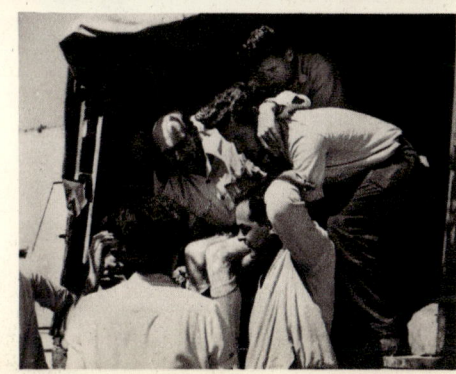

"From Bratislava?"

"Yes! Bratislava!" Young Dvora was recognized by a woman from her town, who had known her older sister.

Her sister, Dvora said, was exterminated. But she hoped her brother was alive, somewhere.

The other refugees watched the recognition hungrily.

"I have my whole family in Palestine!" David declared.

They were given dry clothes. But when Marta was offered a new dress, she refused it. Young Dvora noticed that the dress handed to Marta was short-sleeved, while her own new dress had long sleeves. She offered to exchange with Marta.

"I was hidden in a nunnery the whole time," Dvora said. "I was lucky." There was no brand on her arm.

"Eat! Eat!" Abba said as they came into the big dining-hall.

"From our own fields?" Big Stepan asked, tasting the bread.

"Everything!" Abba declared. "The wheat, the greens, the butter and the honey—all, all is the product of our land!"

After they had rested a few days, he told them, they might go out over Palestine. "The lucky ones have relatives to find."

This David remembered.

Abba stopped two of the girls who were serving the tables. "This too is the product of our land!" Abba said, and he called the girls *sabras,* saying that was the name for children born in Palestine, because they were like the cactus fruit of Eretz Israel—sharp outside, and sweet within.

David wondered how a person felt who was born in Eretz Israel.

Places were found for them, some in the older cottages, and some in the new. Many of the young settlers, like Avram, moved into tents, and gave their beds to the refugees.

But though they had been awake all night, several of the newcomers could not sleep; they wandered over the big yard of the settlement, and they watched the play of the children.

David rested for only a short while. He went out, and there were the children playing; they were born in Palestine, they were *sabras*. Their fathers and mothers were part of the settlement, and came to the children when they were finished with their work.

David's big friend Stepan also could not rest, and Dvora and several of the other young refugees went with Stepan and David to look at the fields and the groves.

[28]

"Everything grows here," David said. "We could live on the roads, easier than in Europe." He hoped that he could get Stepan to start out with him, to search all over Palestine for his family. But Stepan wanted to set right to work, on the soil of Makor Galil.

And Dvora said to David, "We have everything right here. Why should you go on the road? Besides, your family might come here looking for you."

Then Stepan and Dvora talked together of the day when their own group would get new land to settle, and how they would plow! David saw that Stepan was no longer with him.

In the evening, the settlers gave the refugees new Hebrew names, for their new life. When Big Stepan told how he had fought in the ghetto of Warsaw, they named him after a Jewish warrior, Maccabee.

But the sick one, Weisbrod, said there could be no new life for him, as he was of no use for anything. "He is a pessimist," Abba declared jokingly. "A good name for him is Jeremiah."

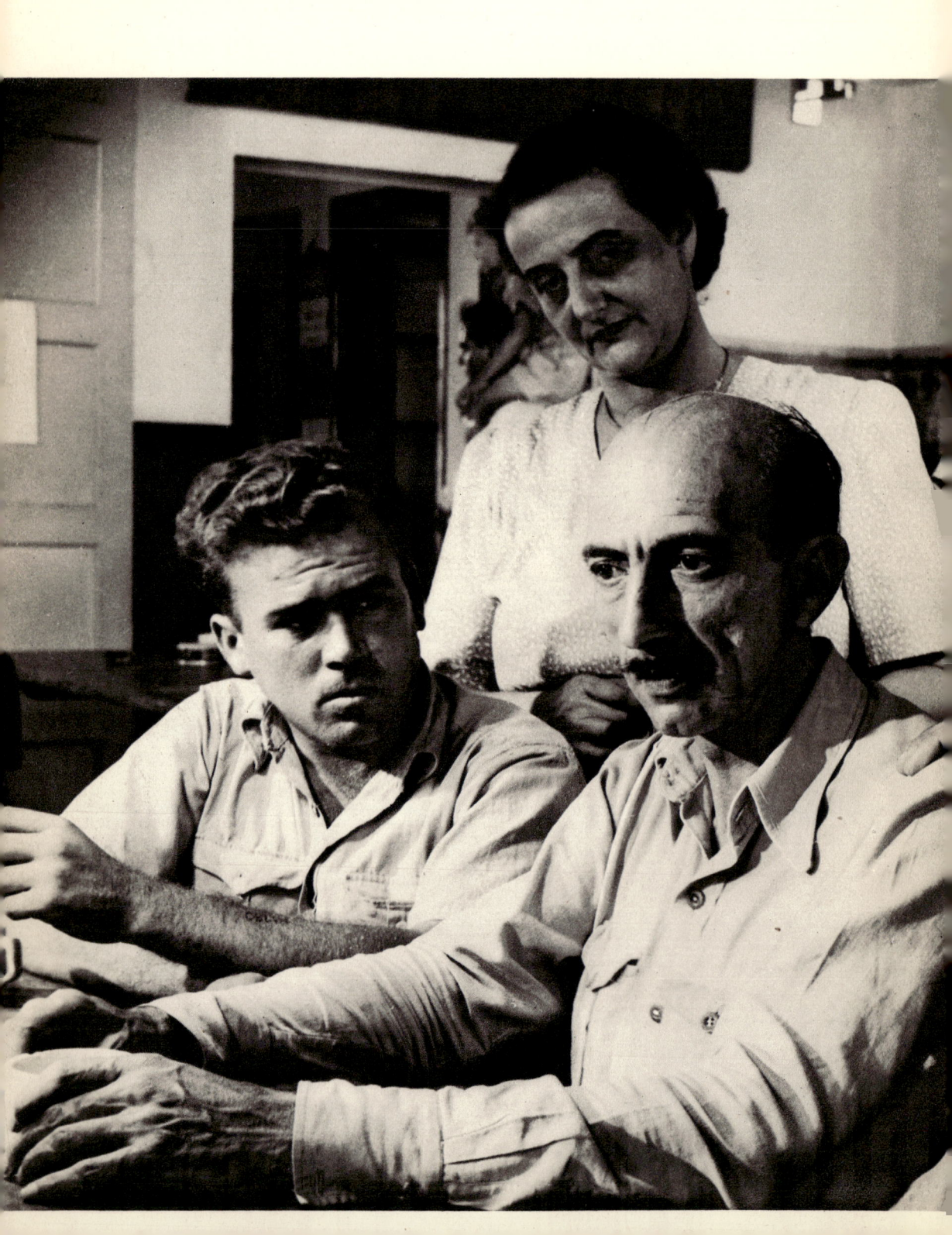

Then David cried, "Nobody is going to change my name! Suppose my father came to find me. He would ask for David, and nobody would know who he meant! . . . When the Germans took us all to a train," David explained, "my father told me to run and hide in the woods. He said I would find him in Palestine."

"But David is a fine Hebrew name," Avram said. "It does not need to be changed." And he told David it was time to go to bed.

Marta, whose name was now Miriam, went with them to the children's house, where several of the mothers were getting their children ready for bed.

Little Shulamith asked if Miriam was the same as a mother for David. "No," Miriam said. "I'm not."

In the morning, David found Avram working in the swamp near the river. The banks of the river had to be cleared of pestholes, Avram said, so as to clean out the breeding places of mosquitoes, which brought malaria, from which many settlers had died.

They went out to look at the big fields of the settlement. One of the Haganah boys who had helped at the landing was driving a tractor. "Don't you want to stay with us and become a tractorist?" he asked David. David did not answer.

"But I do!" cried a girl named Ziona. She climbed up onto the machine.

The others went on to visit the graveyard, but David stayed outside. "I don't like dead," he said to Miriam.

He drew on the ground with a stick. His father had once taught him to write the Hebrew letters of his name, Ha-le-vi.

From his place by the gate, David heard Abba telling how the settlement had first been founded many years before. "We all came down with malaria." Abba said. "Too many died. We had to give up the settlement."

Years later, when his son Avram was grown, Avram's youth group had set out to rebuild Makor Galil. Then Abba had returned with them.

With Avram, David went in to put flowers on a grave.

This was the grave of his mother, Avram said; she had died of malaria in the first days of the colony, when he was very young. David would not listen, and ran from the place.

"Let him go," Miriam said. "He has to learn that mothers die."

By the river bank, David found the Arab boy Mustafa, who showed him how to make a flute out of a reed.

And in her schoolroom, Shulamith prepared a way to make friends with the refugee boy.

She ran out and found him. "Now I am your sister," Shulamith said to David, and showed him what she had done. "And my father and mother are your father and mother, because yours are dead."

David drove her away. "I have my own sisters!" he shouted. "I have my own father and mother. They're not dead!"

David said to Mustafa, "I have to go look for my father. I need a donkey." He offered to trade his American Army knife that he had brought from Europe for Mustafa's donkey.

Mustafa decided to go with David, to show him the way. But when Shulamith went home to wash the numbers from her arm, her mother, Nahama, found out what had happened between the children. Nahama was worried, and spoke to Miriam.

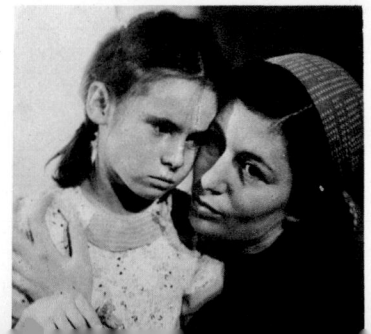

Miriam said, "David will never be able to make friends with the children here. He is jealous, because they have their parents. It would be better for him if he were with other orphans, like himself."

"There is such a place," Nahama said. "A children's village, near Haifa. But surely you would not want to send him away? What would you do without him?"

Later, Miriam could not find the boy.

Miriam asked if anyone had seen David since morning. Avram thought David might have gone to the Arab village.

On the way to the village, Avram met Mustafa's father, Jamal. "*Marhaba,* Jamal," he said. "I was just coming to you."

"*Marhabtein.* And I am coming to you," said Jamal. "Mustafa has not come home with the donkey."

They went together to find the boys.

For a long way, Mustafa and David followed the shore of Galilee. But after a time, Mustafa's donkey halted, and would not carry them any further. "Maybe she is sick," Mustafa said. Then they all walked.

They went up on the road to the hills, and Mustafa said he knew a short cut to the city of Nazareth. But the donkey became so tired, going up the hill, that they had to stop altogether.

When Avram and Jamal found the boys, the donkey had just given birth to a foal. At such a moment, the men could not be angry.

Mustafa wanted to return David's knife, because he had not fulfilled his bargain, but instead the foal was given to David.

"When he grows up," Jamal said, "you can ride him all over Palestine, to find your father's house."

The children were excited over the little animal, and made him a bed, and named him Balaam. But he would not eat.

Then David exclaimed, "He's mine! I'll feed him! I'll give him his name!" But the foal would not take any food from him either.

"He wants his mother," Shulamith said. "He won't eat unless it's from his mother." David drove the children away. And when he was alone with his foal, the little animal lay down and moaned.

Then David took the foal up in his arms, and crossed the fields, and crossed the River Jordan.

"Don't worry, Balaam," he said. "I am taking you home."

He went up to the Arab village.

"Jamal? Mustafa?" he asked. And he found his way to their house.

Abba was sitting in Jamal's house; they were playing dominoes.

As the little donkey went to its mother, Jamal said, "When he is grown, he will leave his mother. Then he will be yours."

David went home with Abba.

That night, David felt desolate and alone, more alone than any little beast of the field. Yet when Miriam came to him, he drove her away.

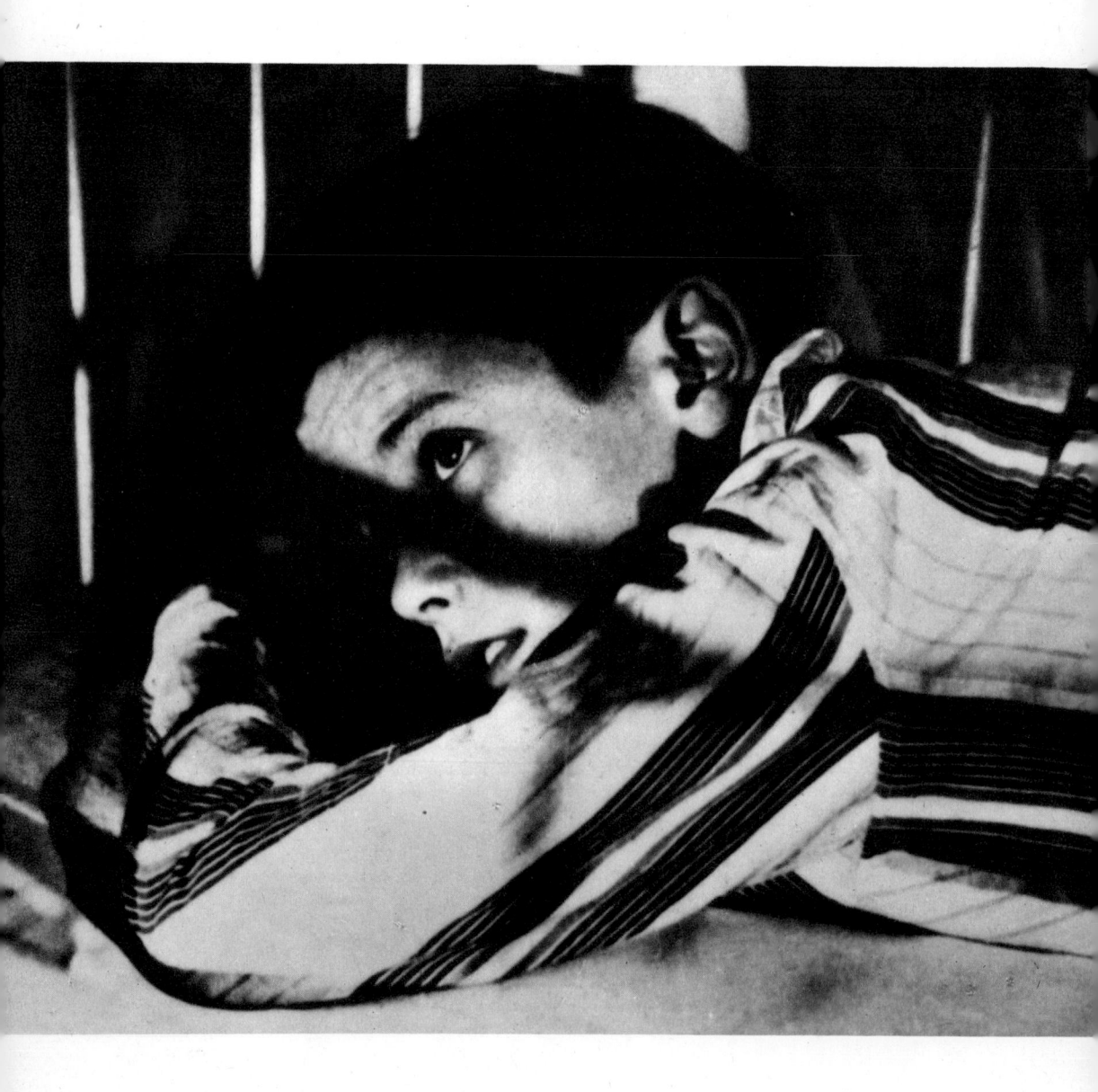

Miriam was convinced David should be sent to the children's village, and raised the question before a meeting.

"All boys run away sometimes," Abba said. "In a while, he will get used to us, and be happy here."

"He is a comrade, a little brother!" Maccabee cried out. "We slept in the snow together, crossing the Alps! Why should we send him away?"

But Miriam would not yield, and at last they agreed to try her plan.

"You will come back to us, David, and live with us when we build our own settlement!" his friends said when he was leaving for the children's village.

This time they passed through the land in the daylight.

Here in Emek Israel, Avram said, the Persians and the Egyptians, the Midianites and the Greeks and the Romans and the Turks had come in their turns, to take the land from the Jews.

And Avram told David the names of the new Jewish settlements.

Then they came to large factories, near a city.

These were oil refineries, Avram explained. From fields in Persia and Arabia, oil flowed in pipes to Palestine, and here it was made into fuel, and put into English warships.

Then they saw the city of Haifa, and the harbor filled with ships.

Avram took Miriam and David to a cafe, to wait while he went to pick up a shipment of DDT, for spraying the swamp against malaria.

While they waited for Avram, Miriam gave David a keepsake—a little comb.

"A man gave it to me a long time ago," she said. "It was all they let me keep, in the camps."

"But I thought they cut off all the ladies' hair," David said.

"Some of us had to keep our hair," Miriam told him. "That's why they let me keep the comb."

Then David drew a picture of his family, as a keepsake for Miriam. There were grandfathers and uncles and cousins, sisters and brothers, besides his mother and father and himself. "That is so you will recognize them if they come for me," he said.

"There is a ship coming in today," the waiter remarked. "Perhaps someone from your family is on this ship!"

They passed through the streets of Haifa, where there were armored cars and jeeps. Avram said the ship coming into the harbor carried only a small number of people who could come in the daylight because they had special papers, given out each month in small numbers.

David watched the people of the monthly quota coming from the ship. There were old people, too old to be his parents. There was a youth group such as he had seen in the camps and on the roads of Europe. There were even a few children, coming together with their families.

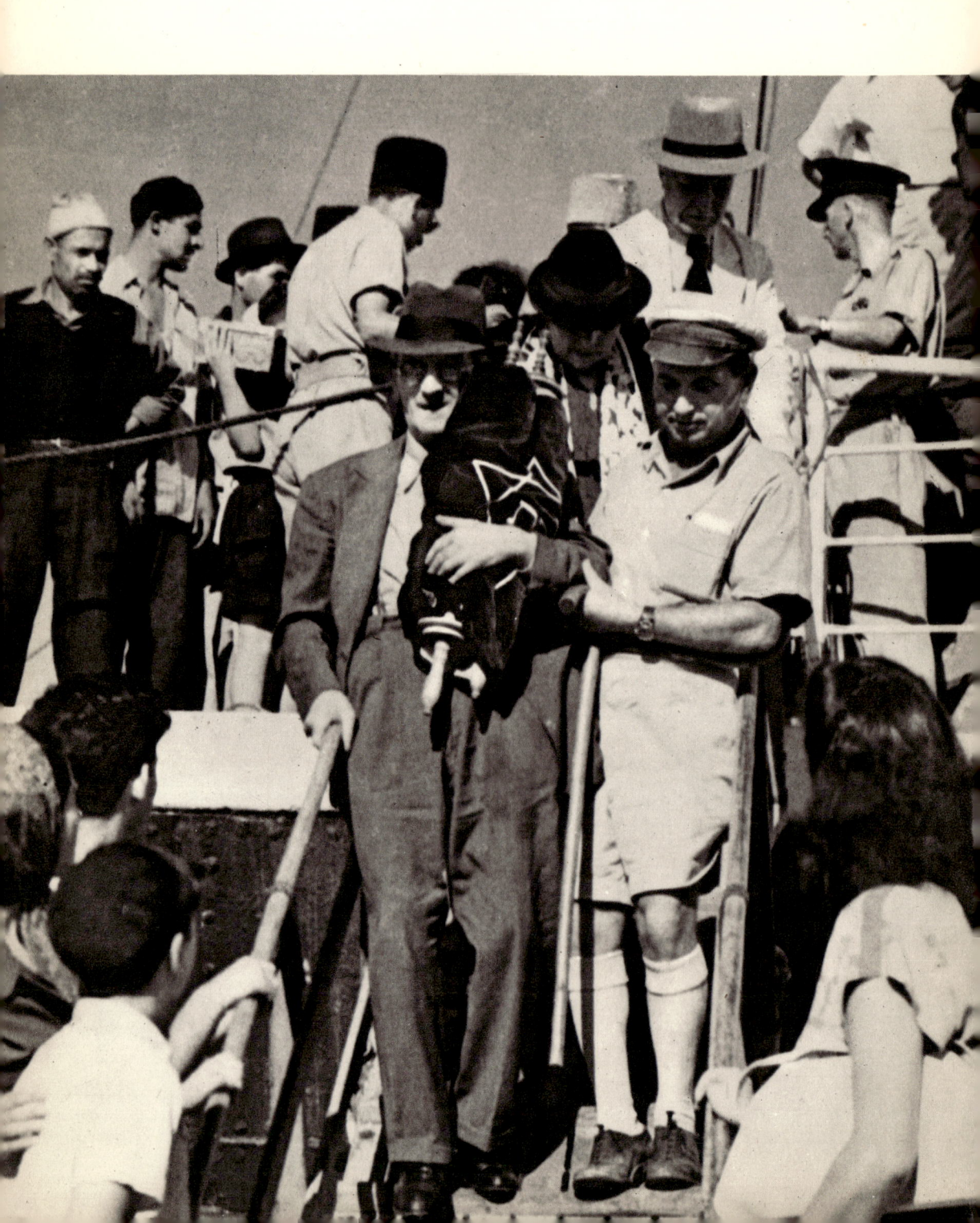

Then, after the old people came from the ship, David saw a man who was of the right age, and looked like a father. The man was alone, and seemed to be looking for someone.

David approached him and said, "I am David. David Halevi."

But the man sorrowfully shook his head, and went away.

Miriam came up to David and said to him, "Many children have lost their parents, David. Even without wars. Avram lost his mother, here in Palestine."

"You don't even believe my family is alive!" David cried out. "Give me back my picture!"

In the children's colony, there were other boys from Europe, like himself. One boy said his name was Baruch, and David said, "Is that your real name, or a name they gave you here?"

Baruch couldn't remember if it was his real name. "The SS just called me *Schmutz*—Dirty," he said.

"I have my real name," David said. "Halevi is my real name, too."

The boys were taking corn in a wagon to the bull pen.

Baruch told how the SS had put all the Jews of his town into the synagogue, and burned them, and how they had caught him watching the fire. But the boy standing on the wagon said, "In my town they couldn't get everybody into the synagogue. They burned whole streets."

"We had a big synagogue," Baruch said.

David told them, "We lived in a city, not a town. So they put everybody into the great square, and mowed them down with machine guns."

Then the biggest boy said, "That was nothing. In Auschwitz, they gave me a job cleaning the furnaces. Every day the ashes alone would fill your whole city square!"

The bull's name was Samson, and David said, "I bet he could break out, if he wanted."

David was given a bed in the same room with Baruch. There was a picture on the wall, and Baruch said, "That's our family in America."

But it was not a real family. It was only a married couple who sent them letters and presents.

"I have a picture of my real family," David said, and showed it to them.

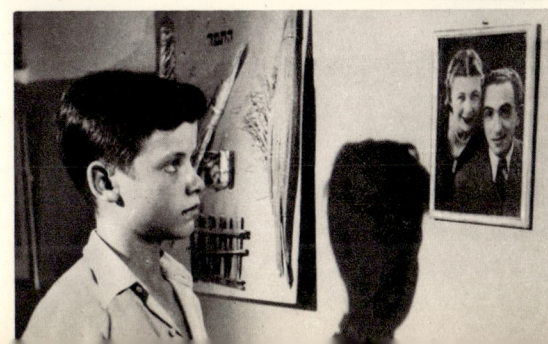

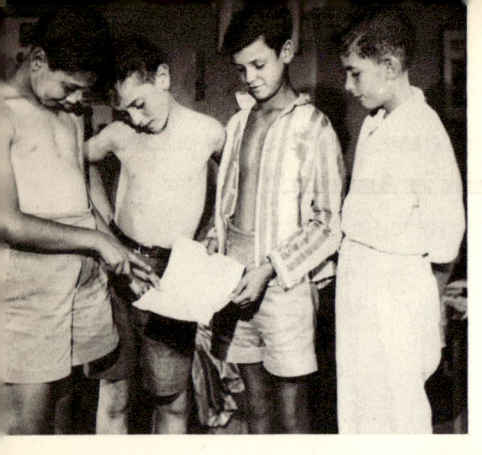

"That's only a picture you drew yourself!" Baruch declared. "We have no real families. We are all orphans. You're just like the rest of us—that's why you're here!"

He seized David's picture. David fought to get it back.

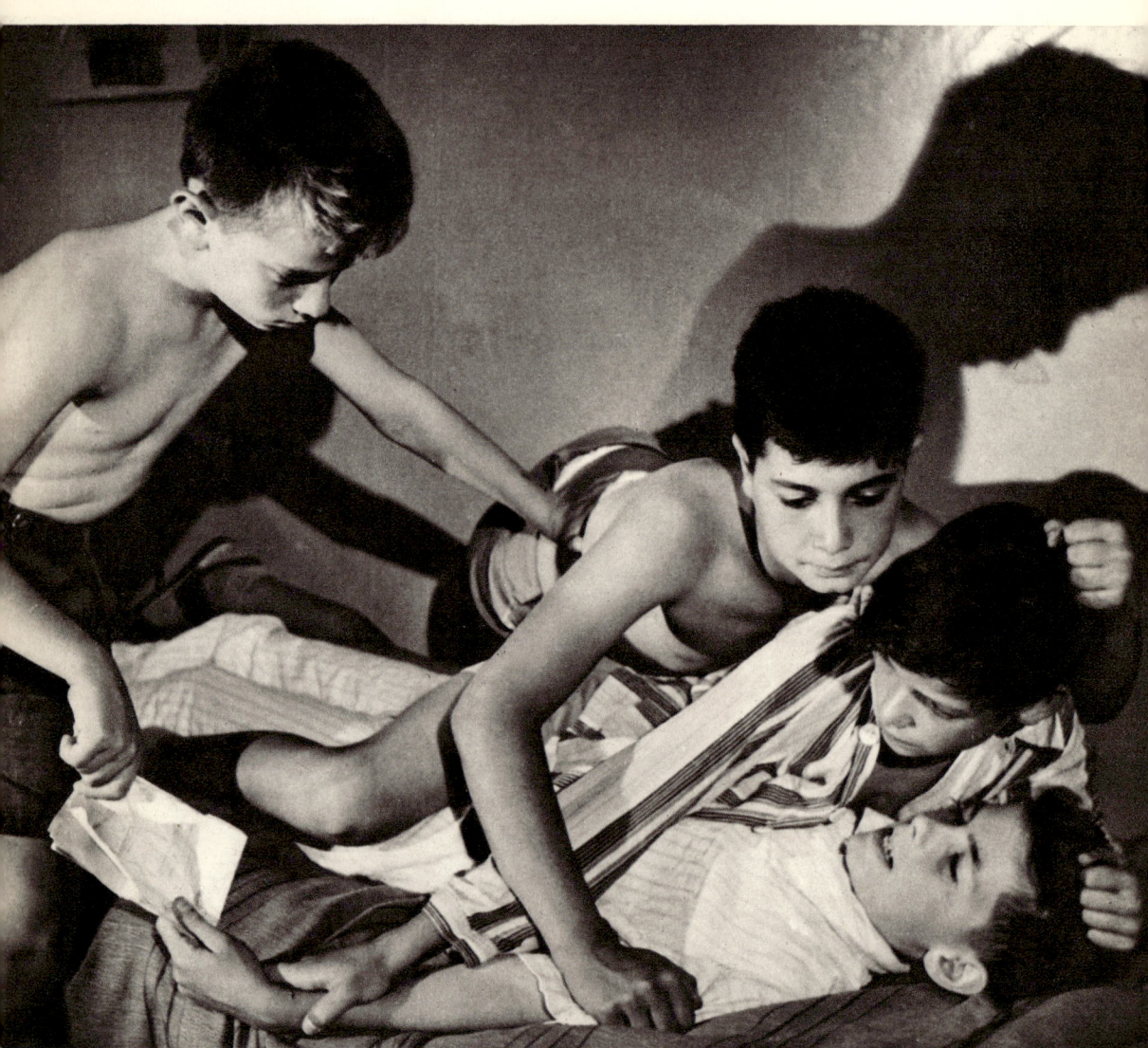

As soon as the other boys were asleep, David ran away, to look for his family. He stumbled over the rocks on the mountainside. All around him jackals howled. He grew tired, and nearly fell, and ran on, and he wanted to cry.

In a small voice he murmured, "Papa, papa."

In the morning, a goatherd found the boy.

['73]

The Arab gave him bread, and showed him the way to the road.

David passed many ancient caves, and wondered if his ancestors had lived in them, and fought from these caves, thousands of years ago.

Now at last he felt he was on his way to find his family.

He was given rides on the road, and came as far as an old harbor, which was Caesarea. There he saw some men who had a car, and they said he could ride with them, as far as the city of Tel Aviv.

They rode along the seashore and came into the city.

The men in the car asked him his name, and when he said "David Halevi," they thought he was the son of a violinist named Halevi, in the Philharmonic Orchestra.

They brought David to the theater where they said the orchestra would be rehearsing.

As David opened the door, the music reached him. It seemed to David that he remembered his father playing on a violin, at home. He had been very small then, when everyone was taken away. He had been five years old.

David asked for the violinist Halevi.

When the music stopped, the man came out to him. But although his name was Halevi, he was not from Poland like David; he had come from Rumania.

"I remember a Halevi from Poland!" another musician called. "He is working at the Dead Sea. His name is Yehuda Halevi—like the great poet—that's why I remember him."

They gave David money to go to the Dead Sea, on a bus.

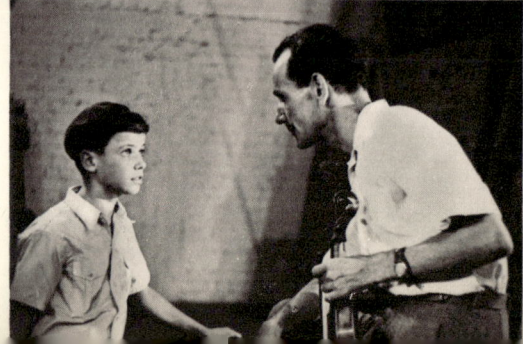

David found the big bus station. He was told it would take only a few hours to go to the Dead Sea.

The bus went down and down into the hot deserted land that seemed to be the end of the earth. Surely if he did not find his people here, David thought, then they were nowhere.

At the end of the wilderness, there was a big factory.

"Why do you want to see Halevi?" the gatekeeper asked. And David said, "I think maybe he is my father."

The gatekeeper laughed.

"Then maybe he is my uncle," David said.

Still laughing, the gatekeeper took David into the factory. "Here is a riddle for you," he said. "Brothers and sisters have I none, but this man's father is my father's son. Who am I?"

The man named Yehuda Halevi was working there, and it was true, he had lived in Poland and escaped. He asked David many questions.

David looked and looked at the man, but at last he had to say what he feared. "You're not my father?"

The man waited a long time to answer. Then he said, "No, David. I'm not your father. I am—your father's brother."

"I've found my own uncle!" David cried. And his uncle Yehuda left his work and took him home. "This is your aunt Chemda. And your baby cousin—Akiba!" he said.

David asked, "Uncle Yehuda, did you look for my father?"

"Yes. I've looked for every Halevi," Yehuda said. And he told of an office in Jerusalem, where there was a book in which the name of every person was written as soon as he was found.

It was Sabbath eve, and the house was filled with a pleasant odor that David remembered now, the odor of freshly baked Sabbath bread.

Then David asked a question that had long troubled him. "Uncle Yehuda, what was my father's name? I can only remember Papa. But how would it be written in the book in Jerusalem?"

"His name?" Yehuda repeated. "Your father's name was Israel. That's how it would be written in the book."

On the day of rest, they went to bathe in the Dead Sea.

Yehuda and Chemda talked of the boy while they floated on the water. "We must tell him the truth," Chemda insisted. "Otherwise it will come out of itself and he will be hurt."

"But if we tell him I am not really his uncle," Yehuda said, "he will simply go away."

The watchman came along with his children, Lami and Reuven. Reuven was scientific, and measured the heat of the sea every day.

"It's nice and warm here. Better than when you lived beside the icy Baltic, eh David?" the watchman said.

But David did not remember ever living beside an icy sea.

The watchman hastily began to play with the baby. "Some people are babies all their lives," his daughter said.

Lami and Reuven took David away to show him a near-by settlement, where water from the Jordan had been brought to soak out the poisons from the arid soil. The land had been dead, Lami said, and now it was reborn.

"Can people be reborn?" David asked.

"That is a theory." Reuven replied. "It is the theory of metempsychosis."

All night long David worried about the icy sea where his uncle had lived. For his own family had lived in Cracow, where there was no sea.

In the morning, he found out the truth. "I told you I was your uncle because we want you to stay with us," Yehuda said. "We are all one family now, all that is left of us, David."

But David said, "You are not my father's brother. He will never come to your house to look for me."

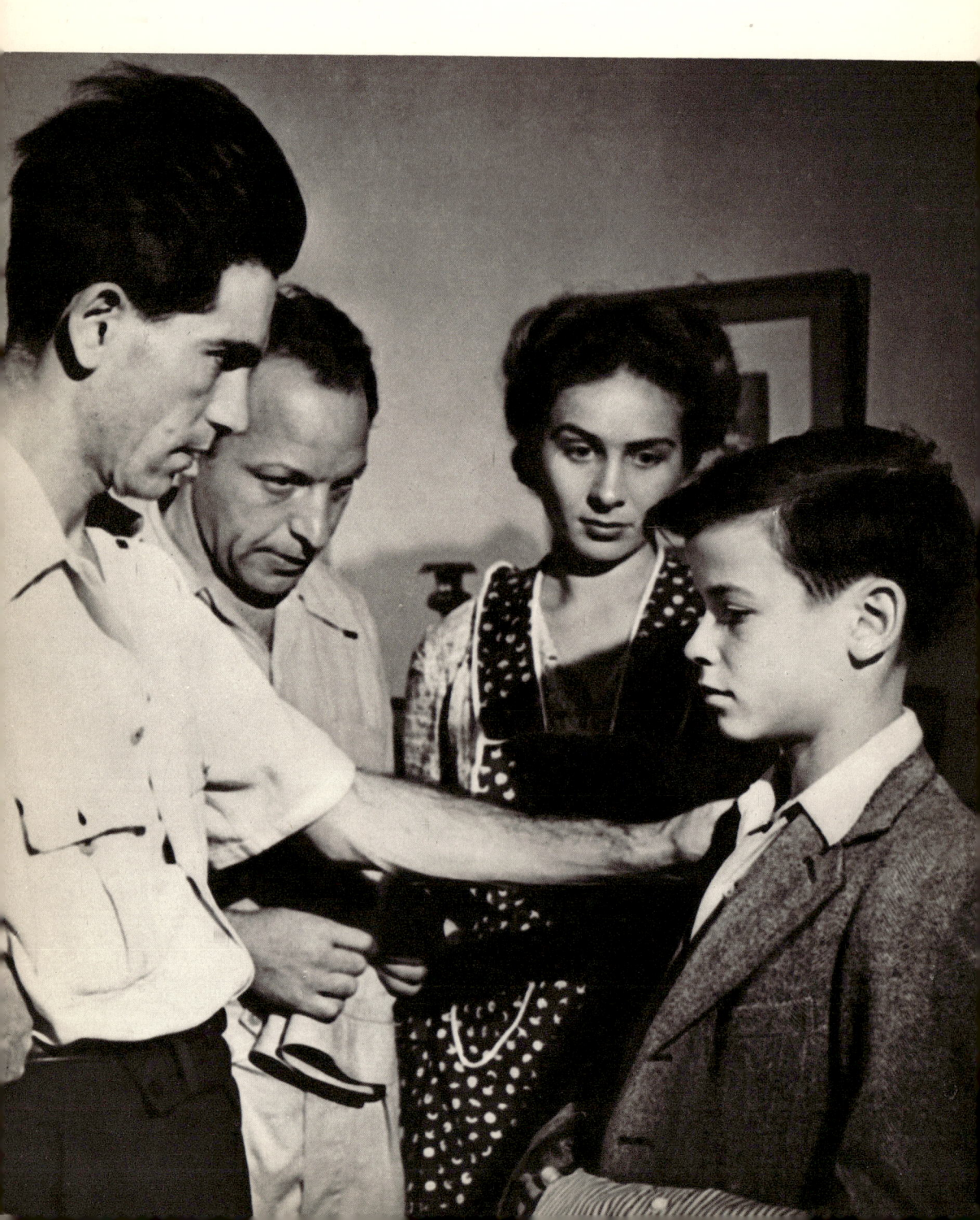

He remembered how Yehuda had spoken of a place in Jerusalem where all the names were written of people who had been found.

David said good-by to the baby, Akiba. "Lucky baby you," he said, "born here."

If he went on the bus, David was afraid he might be seen and stopped in his search. Jerusalem was not far, he believed, and he would find his way there.

The sun was very hot, and there was not a growing blade of grass, for this was the deadly wilderness of Judea.

But at last David saw a watering place.

"Jerusalem?" he asked of a merchant who was watering his camels.

The merchant saw that the boy was tired, and alone in the hills, where one could easily get lost and die. He helped David up onto a camel.

The camel rolled like a rolling ship, and the sun made the boy feel dizzy. But soon he would be in Jerusalem.

Then he saw the city.

[96]

The merchant took the tired boy from the camel and put him on the donkey. They passed the great mosque that was built where the temple of Solomon had been. They passed the garden of Gethsemane, on the Mount of Olives.

They came by a tower that was known as the Tower of David the King.

And they entered the city through the gate of Saint Stephen.

[100]

The merchant told David how to find his way to the new city.

But David became lost in the narrow, turning lanes.

He was tired from his hours of walking under the sun and riding on the camel.

At last he spoke to two priests.

"We will take you to your own people," they said. And on the way, as he told them of his search for his father, they said to him, "On this street, long ago, the Son of Man Himself passed, on His way to His Father."

They brought David to the Jewish quarter, and showed him a door.

David went in, and there he heard a singing and a murmuring.

He saw many old men, and of one of them he asked, "Is this the place where they have the names of the fathers?"

Then the elder replied, "Here we have the names of our fathers in the Torah: Abraham, Isaac, Jacob, Seth, Noah, and all of our fathers' fathers. Are these the names you seek?"

"My father's name is Israel Halevi, from Poland," David said.

Then they told him he must seek his father in the new Jerusalem. They sent a boy named Yitzhak with him, to show him his way.

Yitzhak led David through the ways of old Jerusalem.

From the walls, children called to Yitzhak. They were strange children, wearing masks and beards.

"Why have they got beards?" David asked, and Yitzhak said this day was Purim, and the children were celebrating the triumph of the Jews over Haman, a tyrant of long ago in Babylon, who had tried to kill all the Jews.

"Did he burn them in a crematorium?" David asked.

"There were no crematoriums in those days," Yitzhak said. "In those days everybody was hanged."

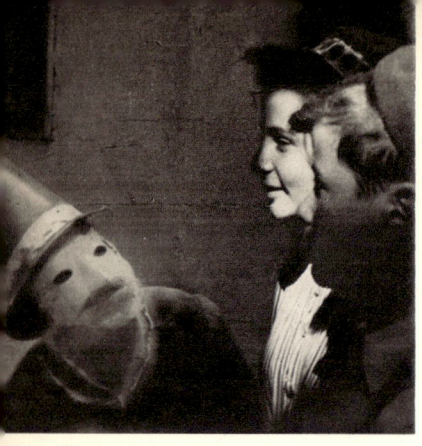

Then the children began laughing, singing a song,

"... hanging high,
Fifty cubits in the sky,
Save us! Esther! Mordecai!"

And they shouted, "You be Haman! You be Mordecai!"

One of the girls was Queen Esther, and she wanted David to play, and be Ahasuerus, the King. But he said no, he could not play, he had to find his father.

"Then I'll go with you!" Esther said, and all the children started running through the streets with them, singing and laughing.

A tall boy, who was the evil Haman, shouted "Hang Mordecai! Kill the Jews!" The children ran and fought with wooden swords, all through the streets into the new city, where they came to a great building which was the Office.

But there a man told them that there had not been room enough for the Search Bureau for Missing Relatives. The Search Bureau was in an old war ruin, across the street.

David wanted to go into the place at last, but Haman caught hold of him, shouting, "He can't go! He's Mordecai, the Jew! I have to hang him!"

Then the children all cried out, "Hang Haman!" And Esther pulled David free, and he saw the ruined place. It was not a ruin from this war, Esther said, but from the Turks, or Romans, or all the wars. And underneath it was whole.

There were signs pointing the way down, and on the stairs there were people sitting, looking in a book that was filled with names.

An old man said, "There will be another list." But the woman beside him said, "If they have not been found until now, they are surely dead."

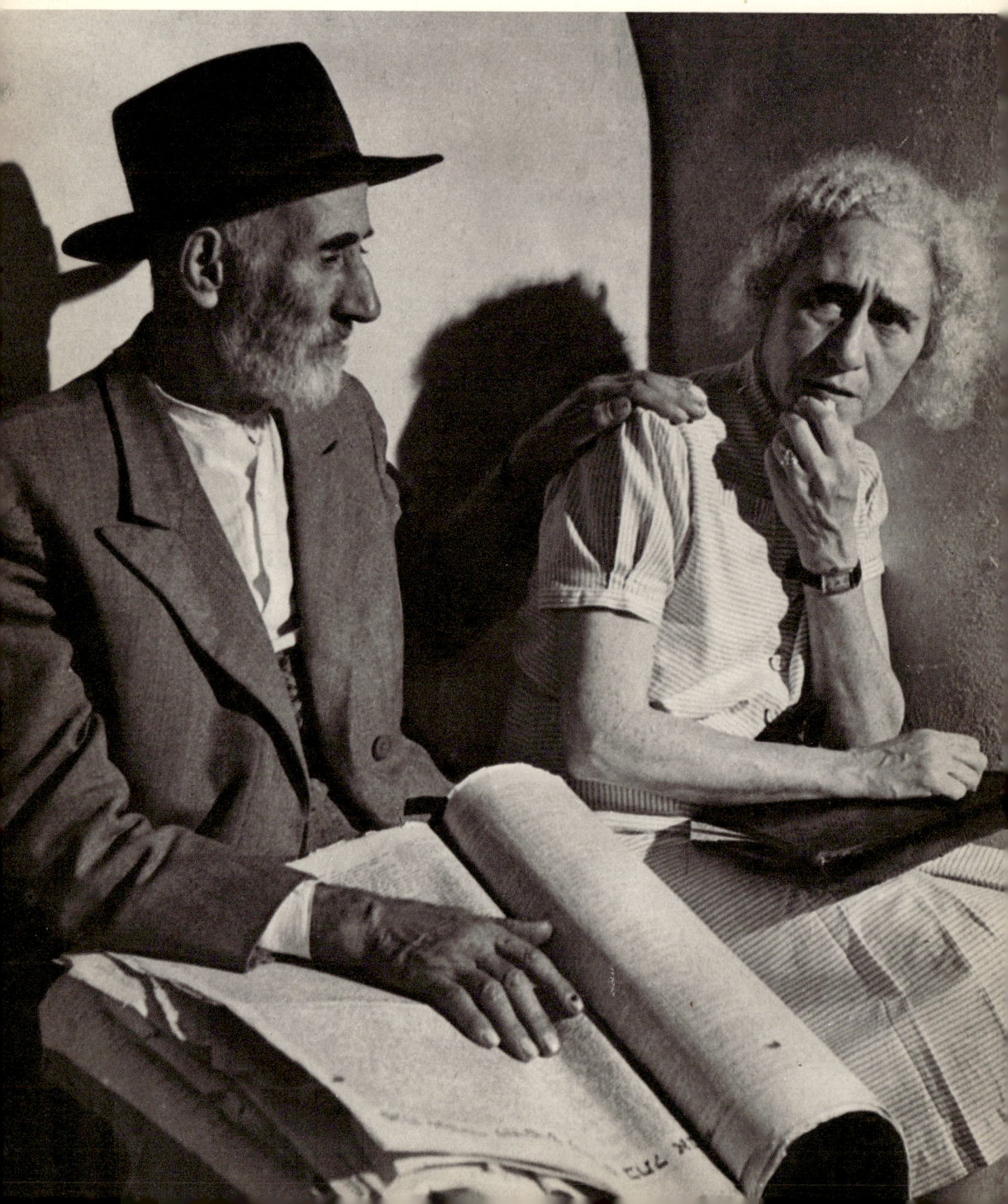

There was an office filled with names. "Halevi? You're David Halevi?" They knew his name, saying there had been a letter about him from Avram, of Makor Galil.

David heard a woman say, "We can't tell him." He could read his name, Halevi, on the papers. "You have to tell me!" he demanded. "What does it say?"

Then the man said, "We haven't found your father, David. Or anyone in your family. Not yet."

"If you haven't found them, they are dead," David said.

The man was silent.

Outside, the children shouted, "Your mother?" "Your father?" "Did you find them?" "Hang him!" "Hang Mordecai!" "Hang Haman!" And a baby laughed and said, "Mama!" And the children shouted, "Ahasuerus! Mordecai! Who do you want to be?" And David felt as though the camel rocked, and the ship rocked, and the cradle rocked.

"He's playing he's a baby," the children said. "For Purim!"
   Then David saw them leaning over him, like fathers and grandfathers with their long beards, and he was happy.
   But Yitzhak said, "In Purim there is no baby."
   Esther cried, "David, stop pretending, stop it!"
   A grown woman came and said, "Something has happened to this boy."

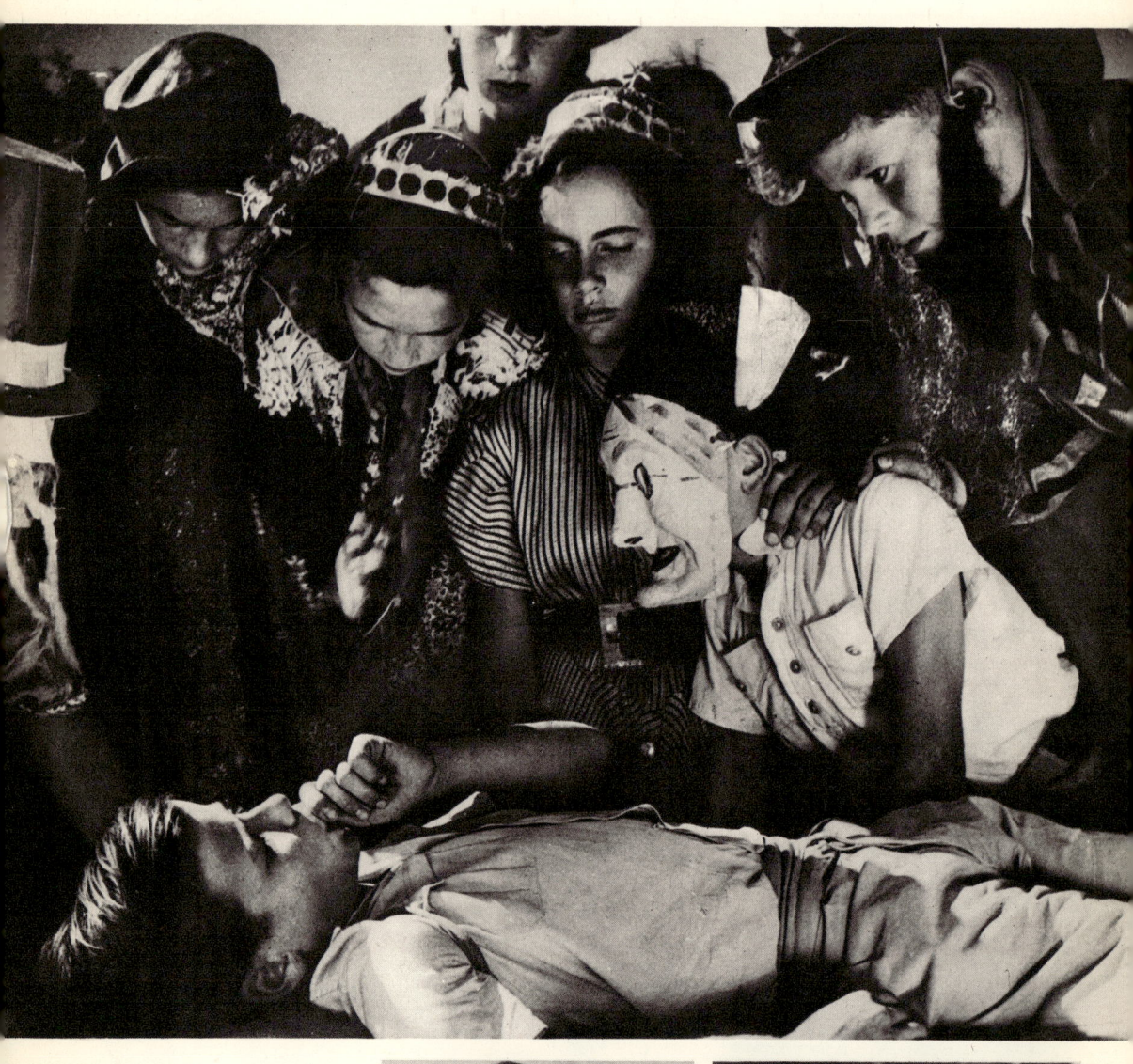

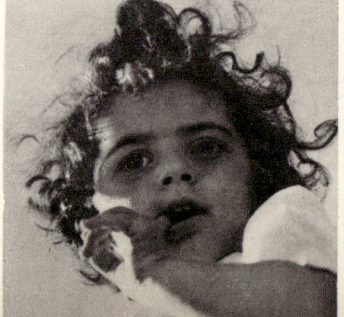

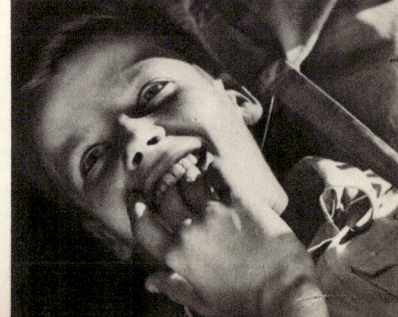

An ambulance was called. David was taken to Hadassah Hospital.

Avram and Miriam had been searching for David and had traced him as far as the Dead Sea. From there they had come, with Yehuda Halevi, to search in Jerusalem.

They found David in the hospital. The doctor hoped the boy would recognize his friends. But David did not know who they were.

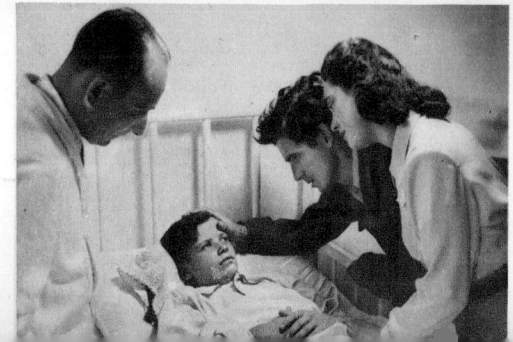

"I will try with deep sleep," the doctor said. "Perhaps it will bring him back to himself. But you see he has found his peace in infancy, and he clings to it."

Then, as they were leaving, the boy called out to Miriam and Avram, "Mama! Papa!"

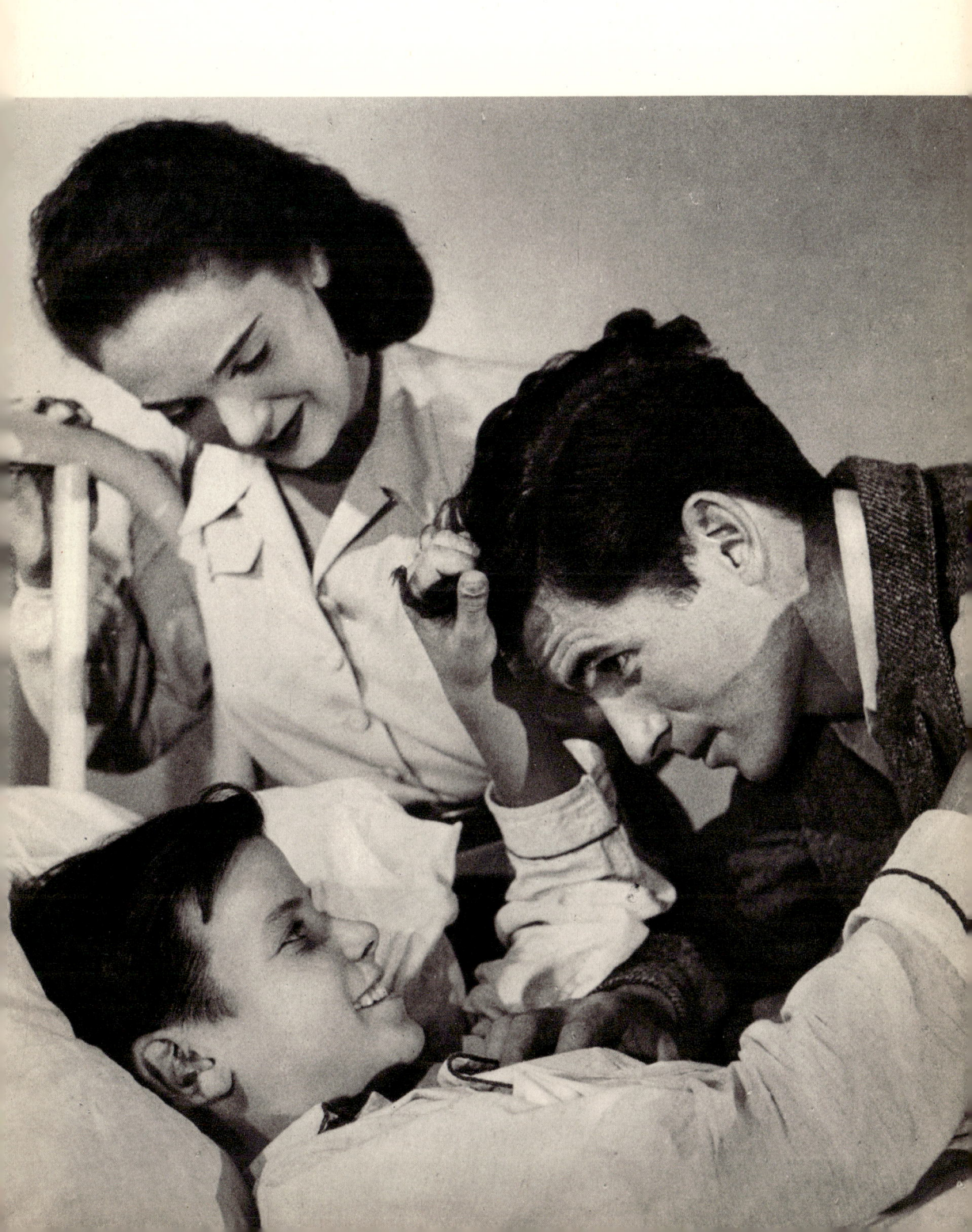

Later, Avram pleaded with Miriam, that they take the boy home with them. "He has made us his mother and father," Avram said. "He will catch up to his own age, and be perfectly normal."

But Miriam kept repeating the doctor's final words. "It is only an illusion. We are not his father and mother. He is not himself. He will be well only when he knows his own self. We have lived too long with illusions."

She would not take the boy again, Miriam said, for she knew only how to hurt him. She blamed herself for having sent David to the orphanage. "I wanted him to give up even the memory of his father and mother, and come to me. I drove him into this!"

Then Avram looked at her and said, "Have you forgotten the really guilty ones already? For David, and for yourself, and for all the others?"

"David needs you," Avram told her. "He needs you to be his mother."

"I can't," Miriam said. She told him she was not worthy of being a mother. She was no longer worthy of life itself.

Then she showed him the mark that she always kept hidden.

"Other girls were able to kill themselves when this was done to them," Miriam said. "I wasn't. I had to go on living."

"With us," Avram said, "what was done with you does not exist. Only what you do with yourself exists."

"Can't you leave me?" she begged.

"I will leave you our child to take care of," Avram said. "He is your responsibility. You will bring him home, Miriam. Our whole life here will help you if you will open yourself to it. But you must come part of the way yourself. You will come. I believe in you."

When Avram went back to Makor Galil, he found that the youth group had received their tract of land for a new settlement. It was in the desert of the Negev, and Avram went out with a few pioneers to prepare the ground.

The group discussed their list of first settlers, which included Miriam. "It's time for her to come home, with David," Dvora said.

But Avram hesitated. Children were never brought out in the first period of a settlement, he reminded them, and as for Miriam—sometimes one person could destroy the morale of an entire pioneer group.

"Yes, she never makes me feel she is one of us," Maccabee said. They agreed to put her on a later list.

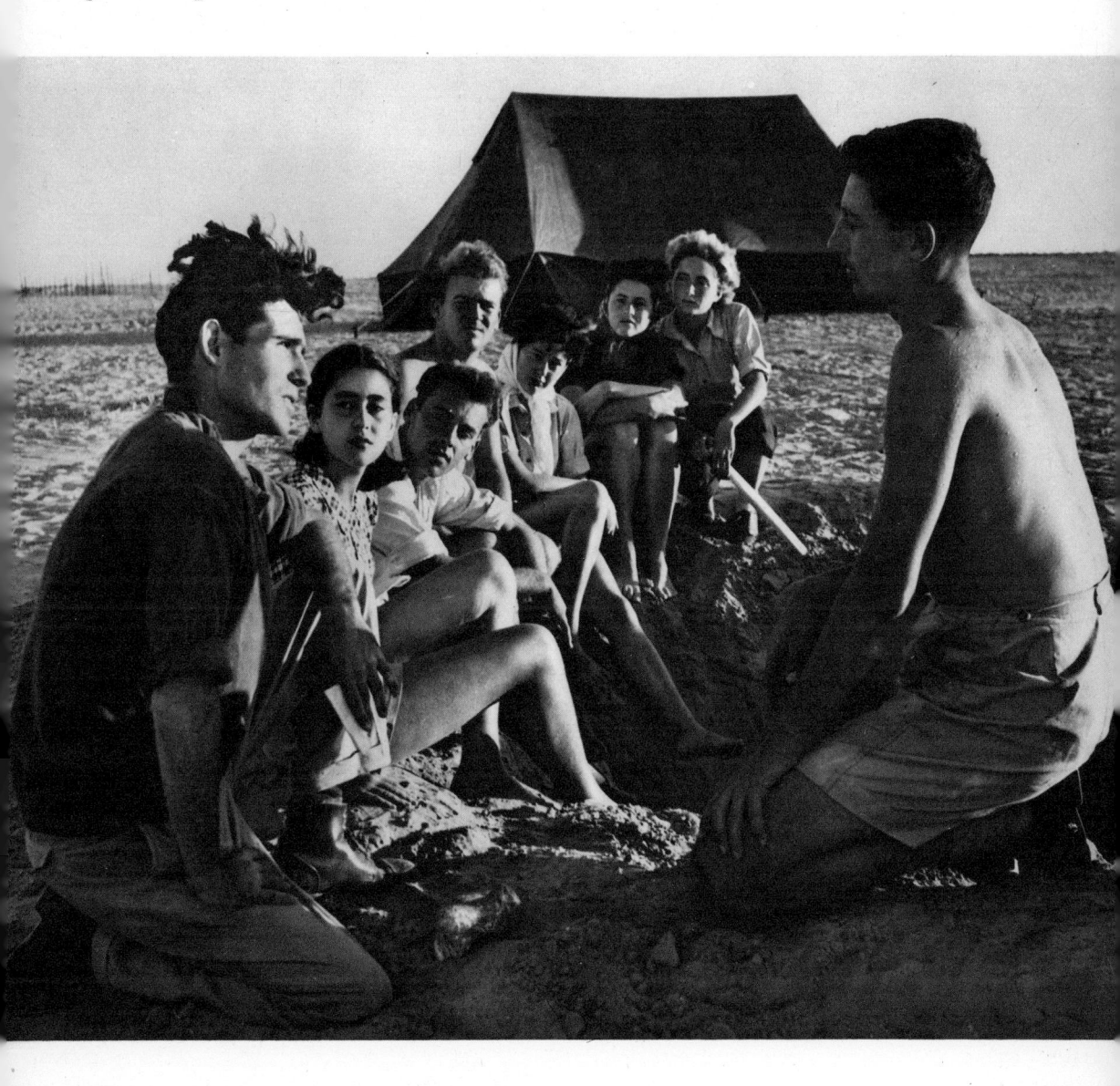

While Avram explored the area, the youngsters started to dig a well, wanting to surprise him by discovering water.

Avram laughed when he found them. They would sooner find oil there than water, he said. But he had located the ruins of an old irrigation system, and had even picked up an ancient household toy to send to David.

"What people lived here once!" he said.

Then the group went back to prepare for the day of building.

Miriam was working at a sanatorium, where she could take care of David. As soon as Nahama could manage, she came up to Jerusalem with Shulamith, to visit them.

The child was slowly improving, Miriam said; he was learning how to feed himself now.

"Don't you think you ought to bring David home?" Nahama said, but Miriam was silent.

"In a few days," Nahama said, "everyone is going up with the *aliyah*—to found the new colony. Avram has even found an irrigation system there!"

And Shulamith gave David the toy that Avram had sent. "It's a donkey," she said. "Avram found it for you, in the desert."

"Avram?" David repeated. "Mama, Avram!"

On the night before the *aliyah*, everyone danced the *hora*, singing,

"*Am Yisroel chai! Am Yisroel chai!*"
"The nation Israel lives! The people Israel lives!"

Miriam brought David home that day to Makor Galil. But she learned that they two were not on the settlement list. "They would take David no matter what the difficulty," she said to Nahama. "It's me they don't want."

"Why don't they want me?" Miriam asked.

"Perhaps, Miriam, because you never let people feel you want them," Nahama said. "Ours is a way of living together, not apart."

Then suddenly Miriam too was pulled in among the dancers.

"Alive! Alive! Israel is alive!" she was singing.

The pioneer group mounted their trucks and drove away in the night to build their colony. Now they were singing a different song:

"Who will build? We will build!
God will build, rebuild the Negev!"

They rode all night, and before dawn they arrived.

They had prepared their houses in sections, and as the day came, they were building.

Amos and Tirza worked on the fences, for first of all an isolated colony had to be made safe. The survivors had no fear of barbed wire now, for this was their own place.

Truckloads of comrades arrived from other settlements, to help the new group in going up to settle on their land.

It was their day.

Maccabee never stopped working, and never stopped eating.

The truck went to Makor Galil, for seedlings and household things. Then Miriam decided to take David to Avram. As they were leaving for the new place, Jamal brought a sheep and a ram for the settlers, and Abba thanked him with the words of Solomon, "A neighbor near is better than a brother far off."

In the new place, Avram and Weisbrod were plowing, and they found stones in the soil. Some of the stones were large, and had been part of a building in former times.

And one stone taken out of the ground had upon it the signs and inscription of the ancient tribe of temple priests and singers, the House of Halevi.

The truck arrived again, bringing Abba and Miriam and David. Abba set the boy on his feet, and David heard Avram call to him, and, for the first time, David walked again.

Then Avram showed the boy the strange stone that had been found.

David read the letters inscribed on the stone. "Ha-le-vi," he read. And he remembered, saying, "That is the name of my real father."

"We will build our house on this stone," Avram said.

And Miriam suggested, "We can call it the house of Halevi."

"The house of my father, Israel," said David.

The Making of the Film *My Father's House*

Production: Herbert Kline and Meyer Levin
Screenplay: Meyer Levin
Direction: Herbert Kline
Director of Photography: Floyd Crosby
Music: Henry Brant
Cameraman: Robert Ziller
Sound Engineer: David Scott
Film Editor: Peter Elgar
Camera Assistants: Rudolph Levy, Rolph Knoeller
Sound Assistants: Sam Greenstein, Jacob Marks, Hillel Vilstein
Editing Assistants: Ralph Rosenblum, George Redfield
Production Assistants: Emanuel Rosenberg, Azaria Rappaport, Chayim Bendor, Sig Rois
Properties: Ayliff Crosby
Scriptgirl: Tereska Torres
Electrician: Chayim Kollander

PLAYERS

David	Ronnie Cohen
Miriam	Irene Broza
Avram	Yitzhak Danziger

REFUGEES

Maccabee	Mickey Cohen
Dvora	Naomi Salzberger
Weisbrod	P. Goldman
Ziona	Ada Marmoresh
Tirza	Tereska Torres
Bentov	Chayim Bendor

SETTLERS

Abba	Herman Heuser
Zev	Issachar Finklestein
Nahama	Miriam Lazarson, New Theatre
Shulamith	Israela Epstein
Amos	Azaria Rappaport
Yehudith	Ora Reiser
Driver	Richard Lehman
Zippora	Kate Epstein
Jamal	Yehezkiel Adaki
Mustafa	Josef Saadia
Waiter	R. Klathkin, Habima Theatre
Malka	Judith Bailin

Baruch	Johnny Loebel
Aryay	Abraham Kamara
Shlomo	Shmuel Roskin-Levy
Tuvia	Dani Atia
Hassan	I. Fischelowitch
Englishman	Stanley Goldfoot
Pincus	Edgar Frank
Violinist	Hans Landesdorf
Conductor	Michael Taube
Smulik	Zalman Leiviush, Ohel Theatre
Yehuda	Joseph Pacovsky, Chamber Theatre
Chemda	Herta Ohrbach
Merchant	A. Nahum
Priest	Rev. J. Tin-Bruggenkate
Priest	Rev. Carlyle Witton-Davies
Elder	Leopold Oppenheimer
Yitzhak	Dan Lefman
Esther	Rachel Levison
Receptionist	Naadia Lurie
Finklestein	Meyer Levin
Clerk	Yemina Pacovsky
Doctor	Dr. Eugene Braun, Hadassah Hospital